W/J

OPERATION SIPPACIK

OPERATION SIPPACIK

Rumer Godden

Illustrated by Capt. James Bryan, RAEC

THE VIKING PRESS   NEW YORK

For Anthony,
who first told the story to me

OPERATION SIPPACIK

Sippacik is pronounced *Sip - ah - jick*

SIPPACIK means "very small young donkey" and that is what she was.

One burningly hot afternoon in Cyprus, in its hilly countryside, Rifat, grandson of the old Turkish Cypriot farmer, Arif Ali, came out into the field where Siyergar, the family donkey, had been grazing alone and there, beside her, under an olive tree, was another donkey, new born.

It was standing on trembling legs, its fur still

damp where Siyergar was licking it clean while its little nose turned inquiringly, looking at this big world into which it had suddenly been dropped. For a moment Rifat stood still in astonishment, but he was only seven and could not contain his joy; he ran and leaped toward them, shouting with excitement, and Siyergar, their own Siyergar, bared her teeth at him and turned her back which, Rifat knew, meant she was going to kick.

He stopped shouting and running. Quietly he picked a tuft of grass and fresh leaves and cajoling, talking, he went to Siyergar, to pat and praise her; this time she accepted him and presently, coaxing and cajoling again, she allowed him to touch the baby donkey. It was a jenny and presently Siyergar allowed Rifat to stroke her. "Sippacik," he whispered the Turkish word, "Sippacik."

Sippacik was not white like her mother; she was black—"Black as mischief," Bombardier Garnett, of the British 27th Battery Royal Artillery, was to say—but she had a white nose and two white patches under her eyes which made them look bigger than other donkeys', more appealing; the eyes were fringed with long black lashes. Her coat, as with all baby donkeys, was

woolly and her ears and legs looked far too big for her; the ears would grow—"a little," said Arif—but a baby donkey's legs are as long from the knee to the hoof when it is born as they will be when it is full grown. "Will she ever be full grown," said Arif when Rifat had run and fetched him—"Dede! Dede!" which means "grandfather." "A new donkey! A baby! A sippacik!" but "Aie!" said Arif Ali. "It's a pity she's so small."

"Small!" said Rifat indignantly. "She's the prettiest, sturdiest donkey in all Cyprus." Rifat never forgot he had been the first person to put his hand on her.

Though Arif Ali pretended to grumble he was really mightily pleased; to have two donkeys instead of one is a big rise in a Cypriot farmer's fortune, especially if both are jennies. The Ali family was poor; their house in the village of Yalova had only one room with a little kitchen room in the courtyard and, under a lemon tree, a lean-to shed for Siyergar. In that one room lived Arif, his wife, whom the children called "Nine"—Grandmother—their son's wife, Suzan, and her two children, Rifat and his sister Nazihar. Arif owned five donums of land. A donum is as much as a cow can plow in one

14

day—cows are used for plowing in Cyprus—so that Arif Ali had a good deal of land but most of it was uncultivated; two years ago he had broken his leg, which had set crookedly, and he could not walk or work as he used to. He managed to sow a patch of mustard, gather some of his carobs and olives, but that was all. "If only Osman Ali were here," sighed Grandmother.

Osman Ali was her son, Suzan's husband, father of Rifat and Nazihar, but neither of the children could remember him. He was taken away before Nazihar was born. "The police took him," said Grandmother, shaking her fist. She meant the Greek Cypriot police.

Cyprus, in the Mediterranean Sea, nearly five hundred miles southeast of Greece and off the mainland of Turkey, is an island of wonderful beaches, where the olive groves often run down to the water. It has mountains, some of them more than six thousand feet high; in winter they are covered with snow. There are dry, rocky hills on which the *runda*, or brush, breaks into thousands of flowers in the spring: anemones, sheets of pink wild cyclamen, ranunculus, orchids. The valleys in summer are hot; lemon, orange, and olive trees, and the strange stiff carobs all flourish. Goats and sheep graze from

well to well and their shepherds play the same sort of pipes they played a thousand years ago just as, among the towns and villages of flat-topped houses, there are ruins of Greek and Roman temples, amphitheaters, and mosaics. There are crusader castles too; but while Cyprus is beautiful and romantic, it has become a land of quarrels.

The people now are Greek Cypriot or Turkish Cypriot and the two do not get on well together.

Osman Ali had been one of the Turkish Cypriot leaders in the last real Cypriot Greek and Cypriot Turkish fight when many people were killed. Osman Ali had been captured but had escaped from the Greek police and taken refuge in Turkey. "If only he would come back," sighed Grandmother, and she argued, "He could, now the blue berets are here." The "blue berets" were the United Nations soldiers.

When "the troubles," as that long, drawn-out fighting quarrel was called, had at last quieted the government of Cyprus had asked the United Nations to send troops to the island, to stay there and keep the peace. The United Nations forces came from many different countries but no matter what nationality the soldiers were—British, Australian, Canadian, Danish,

Swedish—they all wore the United Nations blue berets and served under the United Nations flag, a blue flag with, on it, a round world in a wreath of laurel leaves.

The people of Cyprus were soon used to seeing the stranger soldiers; the blue flag fluttered from posts on the hills, from base camps in valleys, on a house in each town, while trucks and Land-Rovers and armored cars, each with a blue badge, patrolled the roads. The forces kept the Cypriot Greeks and the Cypriot Turks well apart and, "Now they are here, Osman Ali could come back to Yalova," argued Grandmother.

"And how would he get to Yalova?" asked Arif Ali. "How far are we from the sea? Miles! Miles of Greek villages, Greek territory, Greek soldiers, Greek police! If the police catch Osman they will hang him."

"The blue berets. . . ."

"You think the blue berets will bring him in one of their cars?" said Arif Ali. "How often have I told you they must not take sides. Do you want our son to be hung or shot? *Bunak gocagari!*" said Arif Ali, which means "silly old woman."

*   *

For three years Sippacik ran free beside Siyergar in the field while they grazed; Siyergar was hobbled with a rope tying her front legs together, but Sippacik could kick up her heels and race around like a madcap. She would even caper as she trotted along behind Siyergar on the roads, or up the narrow mountain paths as Siyergar worked, steadily carrying her loads of grass or firewood, or panniers of lemons, olives, carobs. Sometimes all that could be seen of Siyergar was four legs going along under a load of grass, sometimes with Grandmother sitting on top. At night in summer the donkeys would stay out in the fields, glad of the cooling earth and the dew after the fierce sun; in winter they came in at dusk to the donkey shed where they could share in the family life and almost put their noses into the kitchen room where Suzan and Grandmother were cooking; very often Sippacik would put her white-nosed face right in and get a fist on that nose from Grandmother.

"Nine, don't. Don't do that," begged Rifat but, "*Huylu eşek!* Devil of a donkey," shouted Grandmother.

"*Güzel eşecik!* Beauty of a donkey," Rifat shouted back.

It made Arif chuckle to hear them; he loved

to annoy Grandmother and, "Well, grandson,"
he said, "you found her. If she is such a beauty
she had better be yours."

"Mine!" Rifat's brown eyes flashed with pride.
Then, "You don't really mean it, Dede?" he
said.

"Of course he doesn't mean it. Who would give as much as a chicken to a bad boy like you!" screeched Grandmother, but, "She's yours," said Arif, and all that day Rifat went around the village boasting, "I have a donkey of my own!" No other boy in Yalova owned a donkey.

*   *

Both Rifat and Sippacik thought these halcyon years would go on forever, but Rifat had been dodging school and now the village schoolmaster, Hasan Dincer, came to complain. "You must go every day," Arif told Rifat. "You have to." When he saw Rifat's disgruntled face, he asked, "Do you want to grow up an ignorant farmer like your grandfather?"

"Yes," said Rifat.

"In my young days there was no school. . . ."

"Ai-aie," said Rifat longingly.

"Osman Ali, your father, was always top of his class," said Grandmother. Rifat shrugged. Arif saw the shrug and gave Rifat a cuff. "You will go every day, or else there will be harder cuffs than that."

Arif was old but he had a powerful fist and

Rifat knew he meant what he said; Rifat went to school, every day, and Arif patted his shoulder and was proud. "That's the way. Everyone has to learn."

Sippacik's learning began too. When Rifat went to school she was, perhaps, bored, because she strayed; a neighbor found her at the far end of the village. "She was coming to look for me in school," said Rifat proudly. "Clever Sippacik," but Arif Ali guessed what had happened and, "She must be hobbled," he said severely.

Sippacik was hobbled with a few inches of cord between her front hooves, so that she had to take short hops and little leaps where once she had frisked and gamboled. She fought and tried to kick but when she kicked she rolled over— she had not learned how to keep her balance as Siyergar could; when Sippacik tried to bite, Arif dealt her a hard blow on her soft nose—he had never hit her before. It was no good Sippacik struggling. Donkeys are born to be hobbled; to wear saddles and pads, to carry panniers, bear heavy loads, to trot when they are told, go tirelessly along the hard roads, up steep mountain paths, to submit. "You are a donkey," Arif's training was saying to Sippacik.

Cypriots are kind to their donkeys; in Cyprus

you do not see donkeys with sores or hurt legs, nor donkeys so thin that their backbones stand out. Cypriot donkeys are loved and well fed—as long as they are good and obedient—and most are so docile they can be trusted; many a donkey has carried her master safely home when he was too drunk to see. They can find their way alone up the steepest mountain path, come when they are called—but Sippacik was not docile, good, or obedient. The stick, which is usually more for guiding than for beating, had to be used in thwacks on Sippacik; once or twice Arif had to put a sharp nail in it to prick her into obedience; he had even to twist her tail which is a severe punishment—an animal's tail is always deeply sensitive. No one wants to do these things but, "She is a Seytan, that one," said Arif—Seytan is Turkish for a devil. Rifat could not bear that. "No, Dede," he pleaded, "no," and he would put his arms defensively around Sippacik's neck, whispering into her furry big ears, *Güzel eşecik, güzel eşecik*. Beautiful little she-donkey." When he was told to tie her up at evening in the shed and she lay down, her legs folded under her, making a small bundle, Rifat sat astride on her back, and talked to her. Sippacik twitched her ears as if she understood.

From the beginning Rifat had had to help to school her. "If she's yours, you must work," said Arif. The first time Rifat got up on Sippacik she kicked up her heels and sent him flying; Arif made him get up again—and again. "No tears," Arif ordered. "Your father's a soldier." Rifat bit back his sobs but he was bruised and sore, and Sippacik had many pricks before she consented to trot quietly around the field.

Like all naughty creatures, Sippacik knew when she had met her match; she learned to bear a light load, even a heavier one, then panniers. She was shod, not with horseshoes as English and American donkeys are shod, but with small steel plates that covered her whole hoof. Soon, with Arif and Rifat, even Suzan, she seemed the pattern of a well-behaved little donkey, and that was what the men of the 27th Battery Royal Artillery were told she was.

*   *

Fresh troubles threatened on the island; there were fresh quarrels; "Incident after incident," said the Colonel at the United Nations Headquarters. "If it's not the Greek Cypriots at the Turkish Cypriots, it's the Turks at the Greeks.

Six of one and half a dozen of the other!" said the Colonel, but the incidents began to be serious and, "If we don't take care we shall have a real fight."

The blue berets were everywhere; towns and roads were patrolled even more strictly, camps were set up near villages where trouble might start, and one fine October morning a convoy of armored cars, trucks, and Land-Rovers came through Yalova. The British 27th Battery Royal Artillery had orders to set up a Command Post in a valley near the village. "The famous Turkish Cypriot leader, Osman Ali, used to live in Yalova," the Colonel had said, "and it might be a trouble spot." The Battery Commander was on leave so that the young captain, Captain Flower, was acting Battery Commander. "You are here to prevent trouble," the Colonel had told him. "Deal with any incident as you think best, but be careful to avoid taking sides. Keep in contact with us by radio."

There were eighty men in the Battery; Captain Flower had two other officers, Lieutenant Thurston and Second Lieutenant Moore: there was a sergeant major and other sergeants, corporals and bombardiers, gunners, signalers, drivers, and cooks. Soldiers of the British army

are good at inventing nicknames—they would
never have called a donkey a tame name like
"black" or "brown" or "white," not even sippacik, "very small young donkey." Gunner Lar-
kin, the youngest in the Battery, was called Kip
because he was always taking a nap and because
of his dreamy, lazy, happy-go-lucky ways; Gunner O'Reilly was Spud because being Irish the

men said he was brought up on potatoes; he certainly had a passion for them, boiled or roast as well as chips, and he was far too fat. Bombardier Garnett had no nickname; no one knew much about him except that he was efficient and he was not popular with the men. "He's kind of dour, sir," Sergeant Major MacGregor told Captain Flower.

The Sergeant Major, behind his back, was Mac or Pipes because he played the bagpipes. Captain Flower—also behind his back—was Bluebell, partly because of his surname, partly for his eyes which were deeply, intently blue, and partly because it was rumored that he wrote poetry.

Sergeant Major MacGregor had been with Bluebell as his sergeant when the Captain was a subaltern—"Watched over him like a muvver," said Spud—and they relied on one another, worked well together, which made things "kinda peaceful," said Kip. All the men liked the big Sergeant Major because he was absolutely fair to them. "No favorites with him," said Kip. "He don't put upon no one in particular. We all gets it," said Kip. They liked Bluebell too—and had a healthy respect for him.

The camp was near enough to Yalova to be convenient, far enough away to be private, "so we're not plagued with children," said Bombardier Garnett. Most of the men liked being plagued with childen. The Sergeant Major and Kip and Spud never went into the village without sweets in their pockets. The ice-cream van used not to come to Yalova—there had never been money for ice cream—but now the van sounded its chimes in the village street, and the soldiers bought cones and cups for the children; soon even Nazihar, who always ran to her mother at the sight of strangers, would walk right up to the big Sergeant Major while Rifat would hang about the Land-Rovers or lorries, with their blue United Nations markings. Sometimes he was allowed to watch while Spud or one of the others tinkered with an engine; sometimes he was trusted to hand things or to hold them. Rifat began to dream about soldiers, dream that he was one—most of all he longed to go to the Camp but that was not allowed.

The Yalova villagers knew why the blue berets were there, and knew the village was being watched. Bluebell spent hours in the café sitting at a table with a cup of the strong black Turkish coffee he had grown to like. The Sergeant Major always said Kip lived in a happy daze but when Bluebell was quiet it meant that he was thinking—and listening. Feuds between Greek and Turkish Cypriots were not allowed when United Nations were in charge but, particularly now, there were often feuds. Soon Bluebell mysteriously knew all about them. The villagers were not allowed rifles, only shot guns, but many of them had rifles—particularly now. Bluebell discovered where they were hidden. "The Captain doesn't let on," said Spud, "but you bet he can speak their blooming lingo."

"Never!" said Kip. "Nobody could. He jest takes it in through his pores."

Soon Yalova was orderly and quiet. "Can't make rings round old Bluebell," said his men. They, and Bluebell, had not met Sippacik then.

*   *

The unrest grew worse, and orders came for the Battery to set up three observation posts, high on the mountain top, on ridges overlooking the roads and fields that lay around Yalova. The O.P.s, as the soldiers called them, were to be manned day and night, "An' what can we observe at night?" asked Garnett derisively.

"We can be on the alert," said the Sergeant Major. "We don't want anyone slipping in or out without us knowing, or a sudden attack. Things are very jumpy now," said Sergeant Major MacGregor.

The Command Post and Base Camp in the valley were near a mountain stream so that there was plenty of water; the ground was level enough to pitch the tents. There were olive trees so that the men could eat their meals in the shade—though it was October the weather was still hot. The men's tents in their sections were pitched in half circles; by day, with the tent flaps laid back, exactly alike as Sergeant Major MacGregor ordered, the camp beds made, kit neatly set out, they looked inviting; by night, the lamps lit, they were almost cosy. The Officers' Mess for Bluebell, Lieutenant Thurston, and Second Lieutenant Moore was on a rise of ground and furnished with chairs and a table. Their sleeping tents lay beyond it. The radio truck was apart and the cooks had set up their kitchen under an awning stretched from a supply truck in which the stores were kept; the pots bubbled away over pressure burners in a slit trench, giving off inviting smells. There were even showers made from big food tins with holes in the bottom; they were hung from a branch of a tree above a screen—canvas wrapped around four poles; one soldier stood inside the screen while another climbed up a ladder with a bucket of water and poured it into the food tin when

the water came sprinkling down. There were
even bivouac latrines. "Proper little home from
home," said Spud—he was happy because he got
all the potatoes he could eat. The men were
contented, except perhaps Bombardier Garnett.

It was a good camp but up in the O.P.s, things
would be different.

There was nothing on the mountain ridges but
bare rock and scrub and a few twisted pine trees;
each post was simply a small built-up circle of

rocks, with a tin shanty hut over which flew the blue flag. The hut and little encampment held four men, their radio and batteries and arms, two rifles and two submachine guns. In the O.P.s the men would live on field rations; at night the posts would be illuminated—"We want the people to know we are there." The men would sleep in pup tents if everything were quiet, but if they had to be alert they put their sleeping bags on the bare ground beside a nearby track and a string was tied from one to another so that, without a sound, they could be jerked awake by the sentry. Worst of all, everything for each O.P. had to be carried up the steep, stony tracks. "Every darned thing," moaned Spud: the heavy batteries, all provisions, kit, and most difficult of all, supplies of fresh water. Even Kip said,

"It's crool," as he went toiling up—the Sergeant Major said he took longer than anybody else. "S'more than two thousand feet in the blazing sun." Spud felt it the most; he groaned and moaned and sweated—the others laughed and said it would make him thin. Even the Sergeant Major lost his usual equanimity. "Steep as the side of a house!" while Garnett's dark face grew darker as he heaved and swore.

"Complain to the Captain, darlin'!" suggested Spud.

"An' see what you get," said Kip.

What they got was a surprise. Bluebell sent a message to Regimental Headquarters, asking permission to use local transport, which meant a mule or a donkey. Presently a signal came back. "Authorize you take on strength, one donkey."

*　　　*

Rifat saw the group of men from the schoolhouse window, and guessed why Hasan Dincer had left his boys and girls in charge of the assistant teacher; the schoolmaster was acting as an interpreter, for there, in Arif Ali's field, were three British soldiers. Then, as Rifat watched, he saw his grandfather come limping across the field, leading an unmistakable small donkey, black with a white nose. For a moment Rifat stared, then he slid down from his seat, crawled along the floor under the desks to the back of the room, and slipped out of the door. Nazihar, who was on a bench among the infants at the back, slid down and ran after him. Quick and surefooted as two little goats they ran across the field to where the men stood, all looking at Sippacik.

Sippacik was now five years old and at five a donkey is full size—"If you can call it a size," Arif used to tease Rifat. "She's far too small," and Rifat always rose, like a fish to a fly.

"Small! Dede!" each time Rifat flashed back. "She's the sturdiest, prettiest, cleverest donkey in Cyprus."

Rifat was twelve now, tall for his age, strong and sturdy, with bright brown eyes and close-cropped dark hair. Nazihar had the frizzy auburn curls of many Turkish women and their dark grey eyes, but both children had olive-brown skins, their cheeks tinged with rosiness, and both wore tiny gold rings in their ears, rings handed down by their grandparents' great grandmothers.

Now Rifat and Nazihar came and stood beside their grandfather Arif where he held Sippacik.

"She's small," said Bombardier Garnett.

"Small!" cried Arif when the schoolmaster had interpreted. "Small! She's the sturdiest, prettiest, cleverest donkey in Cyprus." Rifat could not help smiling and, "She's mine," he said proudly. The schoolmaster swung round. "Rifat Ali, Nazihar, go back to the schoolhouse *at once*," but Rifat only hid himself behind Arif and Nazihar went to her friend the Sergeant Major and put her hand in his.

"She's small," said Garnett of Sippacik again.

"She's gorgeous," said Kip, full of admiration.

"What other donkey is there?" The schoolmaster seemed to be asking it of the sky. "We are gathering the carobs, the harvest is at its height; every other donkey is being used."

"Except this dud," said Garnett.

Rifat did not know what a "dud" was, but he did not like the sound of it, and he glared at Garnett. Kip glared too. "Dud! She's a little smasher."

"She is young, well trained," said the schoolmaster. "Arif Ali trains well."

"But can she carry weight?" asked the Sergeant Major doubtfully, as Kip fondled Sippacik's ears.

Rifat still did not understand what was happening; from his post behind Arif he watched while the Sergeant Major and Garnett examined Sippacik from head to tail, picking up her hooves to look at her feet, feeling her backbone, leading her up and down. Rifat thought they were admiring her and swelled with pride; then he saw the Sergeant Major and Garnett nod in agreement though Garnett's nod was grudging; the next moment the Sergeant Major was counting out money. "Better to buy outright," he had advised Bluebell.

"Yes, H.Q. have agreed," said Bluebell. "We don't know how long we shall want the donkey and we can sell when we're finished. There's always a sale for a good donkey." Now the Sergeant Major counted twenty-five pounds in notes into Arif's hand; the Paymaster had brought up the money that day.

"Twenty-five pounds to include the pad, the wooden saddle, halter, rope, and panniers," said Garnett.

"To include the pad, the wooden saddle, halter, rope, and panniers," repeated the schoolmaster.

"Better include the stick," said Garnett.

Rifat's eyes had looked puzzled from one man to another, but now he understood. Arif was selling Sippacik. His Sippacik! "But she's mine!"

Rifat had forgotten all about the schoolmaster and was shouting. "Dede! Grandfather. You can't sell her. She's mine," but Arif was counting out the notes, his tongue licking his lips. He had not dreamed he could ever get a full donkey's price for a donkey as small as Sippacik. These days things were even worse with the Ali household; Arif had not been able to gather his carobs in time to get a good price—he had not finished reaping his mustard though Suzan had helped him. Arif knew he spent far too much time sitting in the café with the other men but, "An old man should be able to take a little ease," he said. "Not if he hasn't a son," said Suzan, who, with fieldwork and housework, felt as if her back would break. "If only Osman Ali would come back," moaned Grandmother and, "United Nations are here beside us," she argued again. "He would be safe in Yalova, once he gets here," and again Arif answered, "And how would he get here? Do you want our son to be *shot?*"

No one would risk that though life on the farm was difficult without a strong man. To sell Sippacik was a golden chance, but now Arif became aware of Rifat's frantic cries. "You can't sell her, she's mine. Mine!" cried Rifat in a storm of tears.

"Grandson, I have to sell her," said Arif. "We must eat," and he gave the rope into Kip's hand. "Take her," he said.

Rifat caught Arif's arm. "Dede! Grandfather. At least let me go with her."

Arif looked down into Rifat's pleading face, at his swollen, tear-filled eyes. "Would you take the boy to look after her?" he asked. "Ask them," he said to the schoolmaster. "Would they take the boy."

"We have plenty of boys," said Garnett, looking scornfully at Kip.

"Please! Please!" cried Rifat, using the English word they had learned at school, only he said, "Pleess. Pleess, sir."

Rifat and Nazihar were dressed no better or worse than other Turkish Cypriot children; Rifat wore thin, patched, drill trousers, a ragged sweater, and a man's old waistcoat; Nazihar had a dress over what looked like a pair of cotton flowered pajama trousers. Their feet were bare and though their hair was combed it had never been brushed, so that it looked dusty. They did not wash often because there was no running water in their home; it had to be fetched from the village tap. Arif, Grandmother, Suzan, and the schoolmaster saw nothing wrong with them, but to Bombardier Garnett they were dirty, shabby ragamuffins, and he did not want to be bothered with them; nor was he moved by Rifat's tears—Nazihar too was crying in sympathy— nor by the desperation in Rifat's voice. "Let's get on back," he said to Kip, and as Kip swung Sippacik round, Garnett turned on Rifat. "Out of the way," he said. "Git. Vamoose."

Rifat gave a shout of rage and tried to run at Kip, to get Sippacik's rope out of his hand, but Hasan Dincer caught him by the back of his waistcoat, like a kitten by the scruff of its neck, and lifted him out of the way. Rifat shouted again but the schoolmaster gave him a cuff that silenced him. "Be quiet. Get back to school at once," said Hasan Dincer in a terrible voice. "This is men's business."

In a few minutes Sippacik was gone.

*   *

The whole camp turned out to greet the new member of the Battery. "A moke like any other," Garnett had said, introducing her but, "She's dandy," the men said when they saw Sippacik and, "That's something like a donkey!" or, "When I was a kid I always wanted a donkey," and, "Seems a little bit of a thing to carry loads up that mountain to the O.P.s."

Arif had shown Kip how to hobble Sippacik to let her graze but the men decided that was cruel, and she was tethered by a long rope from her halter to a tree, the rope to prevent her from straying. Not that Sippacik had any intention of straying; there was grazing all around her, quite enough to feed one small donkey, but the Sergeant Major had bought a bag of chaff and a feed was put into a wash basin. Sippacik did not eat the feed because the men brought her so many tidbits of apples and carrots, sugar and slices of bread, and their ration of chocolate. Spud even sacrificed a potato. "I'll teach her to like potatoes," said Spud.

"She won't do a stroke of work if you feed her like that," Garnett cautioned them.

"Piffle! She needs feeding," crooned Kip.

"Far too thin!" said Spud.

Kip commandeered a stiff brush and brushed the dust out of Sippacik's coat; Spud painted her hooves with gun oil to prevent them from cracking. Straw was spread to make her a bed, and then one or two of the men got knives and cut her a pile of fresh grass. "Yes, let's hand-feed her," said Garnett.

They were all so interested and pleased that Bluebell felt he must warn them. "The donkey's here just for this Operation, remember. When it's over we shall resell her," but the men were already making plans. "The Paras have a pony for a mascot; the Irish Guards have a wolfhound. Why shouldn't we have a mascot?" they asked.

"A donkey's just right as a mascot for this Battery," said Garnett.

Sippacik stopped her munching and looked at Garnett. He said it was a coincidence but, "She looked at him terrible straight," Kip said.

*   *

"You didn't hear or pick up anything in Yalova about a man called Osman Ali?" Bluebell asked the Sergeant Major when they were alone. "The Cypriot Turk, Osman Ali."

"Arif, not Osman," said the Sergeant Major. "Arif Ali was the old farmer who sold the donkey to us."

"Arif. An old man." Bluebell was thoughtful. "This Osman Ali might be his son."

"Rather a coincidence, wouldn't it be, sir?" asked the Sergeant Major but, "Coincidences happen," said Bluebell. He went on. "Osman

Ali was a Turkish Cypriot leader in the last troubles, and was concerned in the killings. The police arrested him but he escaped to the mainland. Now the story is that he's back—just landed."

"Landed where, sir?"

"Somewhere along the coast, and of course he's being hunted. Did you notice when we drove to Headquarters there were Greek Cypriot soldiers at every crossing, posted outside every village? As you know, we mustn't interfere," said Bluebell. "Next week probably the Turks will be chasing a Greek. No, we can't take sides, but if Osman Ali could reach Yalova, he would be safe. It would save us a mint of trouble if he could get there without an incident."

"Yes," said the Sergeant Major and sighed. "Incidents! Incidents!"

"This could be a bad one," said Bluebell. "If the Greek Cypriots catch Osman Ali he will be brought to trial and probably be hung and that will start a real fight."

*　　　*

Kip saddled Sippacik next morning with the wooden saddle. Arif had shown him how to fit it. Hung from it were two sealed Army jerry cans of water, one on each side. "Seem heavy, don't they, for such a little 'un," said Kip anxiously; "fifty pounds or thereabouts, each."

"I know. I've carried 'em!" said Spud.

"It's too much," said Kip.

"Go on!" said Garnett. "A donkey can carry a hundred and fifty pounds," and he quoted the official figures: "A mule, two hundred pounds; a goat, forty; a sheep, thirty."

"She's not much bigger than a goat," said Kip.

"A flipping big goat," said Garnett.

Kip had found a floppy old military hat in which he cut two slits for Sippacik's ears and crowned her head with it. "S'ignorant you are," he told Garnett when Garnett laughed. "Donkeys wear hats in Italy against the sun; the sun's far hotter here."

Kip was to lead Sippacik; Spud and Garnett, carrying the rations, were going up to the O.P. as reliefs; the Sergeant Major had come to superintend and Bluebell was making an inspection. "Quite a procession," said Garnett. The whole camp turned out to see them start. Sippacik followed Kip, her hat shading her eyes, the black water cans hanging like panniers; Spud, Garnett, and the Sergeant Major came behind her, and Bluebell brought up the rear. Sippacik trotted nicely along the road until they branched off into a defile where she jerked the rope from Kip and snatched a thistle. Then, slowly, in single file they began the climb up the hill. High on the mountain above them fluttered the blue flag of the O.P. Sippacik was a little finicky now, picking her way through the stones of the narrow track, but Kip was patient. Bit by bit the thistle disappeared into her mouth; she looked round for another but the mountain yielded nothing. Sippacik flicked her tail.

The air was clear, the sun warm; the men had nothing to carry but their rations and their packs—"Sippacik can come down and go up again with the batteries," said the Sergeant Major—and everyone was in good spirits. Bluebell had begun his clear whistle that was as good as a march tune when he saw that the men were beginning to tread on one another; he to tread on the Sergeant Major, who was in front of him as they crowded up. They were going more and more slowly. "Hurry. along," Bluebell shouted ahead to Kip. "There's no need to take it as slowly as this."

"Sorry, sir," Kip called back. "But she won't go no faster."

"Give her a tug," said Spud.

"Whack her!" said Garnett.

Kip tugged but Sippacik hung back on the rope; he used the stick Garnett had taken from Arif, giving Sippacik a light tap. "Ar! C'mon!"

said Garnett; he seized the stick from Kip and gave Sippacik two smart thwacks. For a moment she trotted, then slowed, tucking her tail in pathetically as if she feared more blows. "That's enough, Garnett," said the Sergeant Major and, in his turn, seized the stick from Garnett and gave it to Spud. "Give her enough to keep her going," he said. "No need to be brutal." Spud thwacked, but gently. Sippacik looked back out of the corner of her eye to see who held the stick and, at once, slowed down.

"We'll be here all day, at this rate," said Bluebell, and again to Kip, *"Can't* you bring her along, man?" But neither Kip, who was scarlet in the face now from tugging and chiding, nor Spud, who was steadily thwacking, could bring Sippacik along, except by one or two unwilling steps at a time. Then, when the *runda* ended and they came to the rocks where the track showed bare as it went up and up, winding among the rocks, Sippacik stopped altogether. "Go on!" shouted Garnett. "Git on, you lazy little basket!"

Sippacik looked at him with eyes that Kip swore were swimming in tears, her head drooped, and suddenly her legs began to tremble. "You see," cried Kip. "I told you. Them tins are far too heavy."

"Garn!" said Garnett. "A wily, four-legged hussy, a minx, that's what she is. Having you all on," said Garnett.

"We'll have her on," said Bluebell, coming up from the back, and to Kip, "Turn her around. Lead her downhill; then, when she's really going, swing back in a circle and she may not realize she's going uphill."

But Sippacik knew. As soon as her head was pointed downhill, toward the camp—and grass, carrots, bread, sugar, she went with alacrity, her small hooves treading neatly, her tail alert; when Kip led her round, she came, but as soon as she recognized the track going uphill she stopped, "Instantly!" said Bluebell, vexed. Kip tried again and this time, when they faced uphill, Spud gave her a cut with the stick below her hind quarters. Sippacik only tucked her tail in further and trembled. "C'mon girl," Kip besought. The sun was hot now and sweat was pouring off him. "C'mon!" Sippacik still stood still. Spud and Kip and the Sergeant Major looked at one another in despair and, "This is ridiculous," said Bluebell. "We're lower down than we were. We should have been at the top by now."

"Left to ourselves," said Garnett, who had come up behind.

Suddenly Sippacik gave a start, as if she had been taken off guard; with a shrill whinny she trotted up the track with Garnett behind her. Then she stopped and her hind hooves lashed out, catching Garnett just under the knee. Garnett bent double with the pain and swore; while Sippacik stood and trembled, not only her legs but her whole body. "Here, w'ot did you do?" cried Kip. "W'ot did he do, sir?" and Bluebell repeated the question. "Garnett, what did you do?"

"Gave her a prick, sir, the. . . ." Garnett was still swearing.

"Prick with what?"

Garnett showed the tip of his penknife.

"You jabbed her with *that!*" If Kip had not been red with heat he would have turned white with indignation; his eyes were not dreamy now, they glared. "Jabbed a knife into a dumb animal?"

"That animal's not dumb," said Garnett and, "It's not a knife, it's a penknife, and I didn't jab, I pricked." Garnett was sullen. "It's what she's used to," but an angry chorus broke out.

"Ought to have the R.S.P.C.A. put on to you, we ought."

"Jab a knife into a little donkey!"

"Well, I got her going, didn't I?" asked Garnett.

"You will not get her going like that," said the Sergeant Major curtly. "Put that knife away."

"Yes, sir. What are you going to do, sir?" Garnett said through his teeth.

Sippacik's head drooped further, she still trembled. "The load's too heavy, sir," said Kip again.

"Very well," said Bluebell. "Take off one of the cans and see if you can balance the other, and we'll try like that."

One can came off. Spud took it on his back—"Exactly as before," said Garnett—the Sergeant Major and Kip managed to lash the other can flat on the struts of the saddle and the procession started again—if it could be called a procession—"We've been two hours!" said Bluebell.

Though there was only one can now, Sippacik barely moved. Kip pulled, the Sergeant Major pushed. It grew hotter and hotter; tempers were getting short. By the time they had rounded the next outcrop of rock they were exhausted. It seemed Sippacik was too; she suddenly lay down, rolled on her side and, before their horrified eyes, rolled over and over down the outcrop and hill to a ledge where she lay motionless, the water can still tied and intact on top of her.

226772

Kip gave a cry and dashed down; all of them, except Garnett, followed him. "She's dead!" cried Kip. "We've killed her! Her heart's burst!"

Even Bluebell was perturbed by the stillness but when they reached her Sippacik was simply lying as if waiting for them to come, her eyes accusing.

"If she's broken her leg . . . her leg or her back." Kip was incoherent. "She was too small for that great load! I knew it. I knew it." But when the water can was lifted off, then the saddle, and Bluebell's gentle hands went over her, nothing could be found wrong with Sippacik except a small cut on one hind leg.

"Did she do it a'purpose?" asked Spud.

Sippacik was helped upright, and though she trembled she could stand. The Sergeant Major and Kip moved her a foot or so on the track; "She can walk," said Kip, relieved, but Sippacik tottered on the path, obviously a very ill and shaken little donkey and again she looked at them with those great accusing eyes.

"Stay with her until she has recovered," Bluebell said to Kip. "Then head her back to camp. We'll go on up. Garnett, you carry the second can."

"Are you sure, sir," asked Garnett, "you don't want me to carry the donkey?"

As soon as Kip turned Sippacik campward she trotted quite blithely, but when she came in sight of the tents she slowed down. Whether the cut hurt her more on the level, Kip never knew, but she started to limp and in the camp once more she did "her trembling act," as Garnett called it when he heard. "Been a n'accident?" asked the men, running out and, "Poor little critter! Poor old moke!"

Sippacik was rubbed down—"as if she were a flipping race horse," said Garnett afterward—her cut was dressed from the first-aid kit. She was given water and, as they had no grain, the Quartermaster Sergeant issued some Quaker Oats which the cooks made into porridge, sweetening it with sugar. "Sugar's good for shock." Sippacik liked it very much.

*   *

For six days Sippacik stayed in the camp while the men carried the water, the stores, and heavy batteries up and down to the O.P.s. "Well, sir, her leg's swelled," the Sergeant Major reported. "It's swelled."

"By an infinitesimal amount," said Bluebell. "Better wait till it's healed, sir."

"I'm not going up the mountain with that animal again," said Spud, but he still gave her potatoes. The porridge had become a daily feed; the men saved all their sugar lumps. Sippacik grew plumper and plumper. Bluebell, sitting in his canvas chair outside the Officer's Mess, eyed her thoughtfully. Then he sent for the Sergeant Major.

"Is the donkey better?" The Sergeant Major noticed Bluebell did not call her Sippacik.

"Better? In what way, sir?" The Sergeant Major was hedging and Bluebell knew it.

"Her leg," he said.

"Yes, sir. It's healed."

"Will she go up the mountain?"

"I couldn't say, sir." The Sergeant Major's face was bland. "I couldn't say."

"You could," said Bluebell's expression. "You know she won't go up for us," and he said aloud, "That donkey is here as transport. If she's not transport, she must be changed."

"Changed?" The Sergeant Major hedged again. "Did you say changed, sir?"

"Yes," said Bluebell.

The two men exchanged glances, then, "It's the way the men have taken to her," the Ser-

geant Major explained. "It's made all the differ-
ence out here where they are bored. She's something for them to think about, sir, a pet."

"She's transport," said Bluebell. "Go to the
village and bring that farmer here."

"And Sergeant Major," he said as the Sergeant
Major was going, "keep your ears and eyes
pricked for any sign of that man."

Bluebell had lowered his voice and the Sergeant Major did too as he asked, "Osman Ali?"

Bluebell nodded. "They say he has been shot."

"Then perhaps he's dead, sir."

"It would be hard to kill Osman Ali. No, I
think he's somewhere near, making for home
and the Greek Cypriots know it. A party of them
were found, setting up a check point near Yalova.
We managed to get them to dismantle it. They
are on to something though they said it was only
routine."

"Odd time and place to choose if it's just
routine," said the Sergeant Major.

"Yes," said Bluebell and he added, "I'm pretty
sure Osman Ali is somewhere near."

*   *

When the Land-Rover drove into the village, Arif Ali was not at home. At long last, with Suzan's help, he had finished picking his carobs and had loaded them onto Siyergar and two borrowed donkeys to take them into the carob depot in the town, nine miles away. He would not be back until nightfall and Suzan fell into a panic when she saw the Sergeant Major, Spud, and the schoolmaster in the courtyard. Grandmother was no help; she quickly veiled herself with her black head veil and kept up her perpetual moan, "If only our son were here."

"Please," Suzan begged Hasan Dincer, when he had told the story of Sippacik on the mountain, "please, please don't let them send the donkey back." If Sippacik were returned, all the lovely money would be taken away—there was no disputing with an United Nations Sergeant Major—and, "Please," begged Suzan frantically.

"But how can they keep her if she won't work?" said the schoolmaster.

"Let them take Rifat," begged Suzan. "She'll work for him. Rifat can stay in the camp—he won't eat much, sir," she said to the Sergeant Major. "Rifat will make the donkey go. She always goes best for him. It won't be for long,"

she said, turning to Hasan Dincer, "and when he gets back he will work twice as hard."

The schoolmaster gave a disbelieving snort.

"I swear he will," cried Suzan, wringing her hands. "If not, Arif will beat him, but of your kindness let Rifat go with the soldiers. We have so little, little money. Of your kindness. . . ."

At last Hasan Dincer consented.

There was no need to make up a bundle for Rifat because he had nothing to bring; he had no pajamas because he slept in his clothes and he did not own a toothbrush or a wash cloth or a comb. "We'll fix him up," said the Sergeant Major.

Rifat could not believe it when he was ordered out of school and told to get up into the Land-Rover. "A Land-Rover!" cried the other children. He was to go with the soldiers. "To the camp!" he cried. "The camp!" "Aie! Aie! Aie!" said all the other boys in envy. "Be a man now," the schoolmaster told him. "Give no trouble and make the donkey go. Be strong." Rifat threw out his chest as he stood in the Land-Rover; his eyes glowed. "She'll go for me," he said exultantly.

He did not feel quite so confident when he

stood before Bluebell in the tent. Had Sippacik been up to real mischief? Was there something really wrong? Rifat could not keep his eyes from straying to the wonders of the camp: the trucks and tents with their neat beds: the big radio truck: the smell of cooking that came out from under the awning: the guns: but Bluebell's deep-blue gaze was stern and penetrating and Rifat felt himself quail. Yet when he was taken to Sippacik he could not see anything wrong. Sippacik, tethered to her tree, seemed fat and well, fatter and sleeker than he had ever seen her before; a fresh, green cabbage leaf hung out of her mouth. She did not give Rifat so much as a whinny.

"Load her up," said Bluebell to Kip. "Two water cans, exactly as before." Sippacik rolled an eye at Rifat and dropped the cabbage leaf.

The wooden saddle came out, two cans of water were hung, Rifat watched; it all seemed perfectly normal to him. Then Bluebell took the rope and gave it to Rifat. "Donkey go up there," said Bluebell, pointing up, up to the first O.P. "Up there." Rifat looked up too and was puzzled. Why was the Captain making such a to-do about it? "Donkey go." Why not? thought Rifat, puzzled.

He took the stick from Kip, led Sippacik out on the road and down the defile. Kip, Spud, Bombardier Garnett, the Sergeant Major, and Bluebell followed. At the end of the defile Sippacik stopped, looking up the steep track. Rifat wound the rope round her neck; it was better to let her go up herself, and when she did not move he gave her a thwack. She went on slowly, too slowly for Rifat; he took a nail out of his pocket and fitted it into a notch in the stick. "See!" cried Garnett. "See!"

One prick was enough; Sippacik knew Rifat when he had that nail. She bounced away and next minute she was trotting merrily upward. Not only that, Rifat ran after her and jumped on her back, "On top of the water tins!" cried Kip. "It's too much. It's crool," but Sippacik's legs were not trembling; they went on steadily up. It was true that her trot slowed to a walk when they came to the steep rocks and Rifat slid to the ground but up and up she went with never a falter. The men had all the work they could do to keep up. It was only when they came out on the flat rock under the pine marking the O.P. that Rifat and Sippacik stopped. Sippacik's sides were heaving—she had put on far too much weight—she blew a little through

her white nose, but otherwise she was perfectly composed and Rifat's dark eyes, looking up at Bluebell, said plainly, "What was the trouble?"

"Well, I'll be blowed," said Kip.

"Yes, we're made to look proper silly by one small boy," said Garnett.

"Not silly; brought back to our senses," said Bluebell.

*   *

In the camp Rifat and Sippacik seemed to have changed places. They both had porridge but it was Rifat now who had most of the sugar lumps and chocolate; he would not let the men give much to Sippacik, "Only carrots," he said firmly —Rifat did not like carrots. When the truck went back to Headquarters for stores and rations, the men clubbed together and bought Rifat new shorts and a shirt and a fine red sweater. He put them on with pride but he still wore his old waistcoat. Spud washed his hair in a bucket and showed him how to use a shower but Rifat did not care for that very much. He had a camp bed and a blanket and food four times a day: breakfast, dinner, tea, and supper—he had never come across a meal like tea before—"And be careful not to give him sausages of ham or bacon," said the Sergeant Major. "He's a little Moslem and mustn't eat pig meat." Turkish Cypriots kept strictly to that though many of them drank the local brandy. Much to Spud's amazement Rifat did not like potatoes—except chips; he gorged himself on chips.

It was not surprising then that on the afternoon of his third day in the camp, Rifat felt sleepy. At home he would have had a bit of bread for his midday dinner, with a lump of goat cheese or some beans or a few olives; now and again Grandmother would make a pilaf of vegetables and rice; once a month, perhaps, there would be meat. In the camp that day dinner had been stewed steak and chips, jam roll and tea. Rifat had had three helpings of everything except the tea.

When dinner was over he had had to toil up to the highest of the O.P.s with Garnett, who was not a pleasant companion. Rifat was trusted now to bring Sippacik down again on his own, and "Git along back," ordered Garnett. "No loitering." Rifat did not know what the English word "loitering" meant, but Garnett's tone made him want to do just that. He was, too, overcome with sleep and felt he must stretch out on a rock for a few minutes. I'll just close my eyes, thought Rifat, and he lay down on one of the sun-warmed rocks, holding Sippacik's rope. As soon as Sippacik saw he was fast asleep, she twitched the rope out of his hand.

It was only a few minutes—people who look after animals get a kind of third eye, an instinct that tells them when an animal has strayed, and Rifat suddenly sat bolt upright and looked around for Sippacik. She had gone quite a way, to where a patch of grass showed above an outcrop of rock, rock so heavy and overhanging it made a hollow like a cave. "Seytan!" said Rifat and scrambled over the stones and furze to get her. He caught her quite easily and, for a moment, sat on the grass to let her graze while the sleep cleared from his eyes.

"Hsst!"

Rifat jumped almost out of his skin. A dark face was looking up at him from below the rock, a man's face; a face that was thin and fierce as a hawk but drawn with lines of pain. A stained rag was tied around the head; the khaki shirt was torn open, the trousers ripped and stained, too—with blood, thought Rifat. He could feel his own heart beating.

"Come here," the man said in Turkish. Rifat

70

hesitated. "Come, I won't hurt you, boy," and, "I'm not afraid," said Rifat, though his legs trembled. He slipped from the rock and came nearer, remembering to hold Sippacik. The man was lying on his side and Rifat saw he had dragged himself from under the rock where he had been hidden. "Come closer." Rifat came and knelt, looking into the ravaged face. A peculiar smell came from the man and flies buzzed on his torn trouser leg, and—that's where he is wounded, thought Rifat.

"Boy, where do you live? Whisper." The man's voice was peremptory. He was used to command.

"In Yalova," whispered Rifat.

"Yalova!"

"Yes," whispered Rifat.

"What are you doing here?"

"Working for the British." Rifat jerked his head toward the camp.

"What is your name? Whisper."

"Rifat Ali."

"Rifat Ali!" For a moment the face lit up. "Son of Osman Ali, grandson of Arif?"

"Yes."

"Let me look at you."

The black eyes looked at Rifat hungrily; they

were as penetrating as Bluebell's blue ones. Then, "I think you are a brave boy and well grown," said the man. "And they, are they well too? The old man and woman?" A pause, "Suzan? The baby girl, little Nazihar?"

"She's not a baby now," said Rifat. A tide

of excitement was rising in him. This man knew Nazihar, Arif, Grandmother, Suzan! "Are you . . . are you. . . . ! Then you are Osman Ali, my father," said Rifat.

"Sssh! Come close."

Rifat came so close that the smell was all

around him but he did not care. His father! "I'm wounded," said Osman Ali. "I cannot walk. Son, you must help."

Rifat nodded solemnly. "Can you get me food and water—water above everything? My water bottle is empty and, son, get me a rifle."

"I will get you food," said Rifat slowly. There was plenty of food in the camp—they even gave it to Sippacik—"But I can't get you a rifle. I am working for the British and they trust me," said Rifat. "Besides," he added, looking at the helpless man, "you couldn't use it if I did."

"I could use it on myself," but Osman Ali did not say that. He put out his hand and pressed Rifat's shoulder. "You are a man, son."

*　　　*

"Caught the boy stealing, sir," said Garnett. "Caught him red-handed." Garnett's voice was triumphant, as if he said, "I told you so."

He had brought Rifat to Bluebell's tent, holding him by the collar of his shirt and sweater. "Show the Captain," he ordered and, with his other hand, rolled Rifat's new sweater up; clasped under the sweater, hidden by the swinging waistcoat, were slices of bread, cheese, chocolate, an orange, cigarettes, and an old army water bottle. "He should be sent back to the village in disgrace, sir," said Garnett virtuously. "After *all* we've given him! Blistering little thief!"

"I expect he wanted them for his family," said Bluebell, but his eyes were on that old army water bottle. He put out his hand; took it, examined it, and gave it back. Then he said firmly to Rifat—for Garnett's benefit—"No more! You understand. No more!" then to Garnett, "All right, Bombardier. Let him go."

"Let him go. *With those?*"

"This once. I have cautioned him," and as Rifat fled, Bluebell said, "Garnett, have you ever known what it is to be hungry?" After a moment he ordered, "Send Sergeant Major Mac-Gregor to me."

When the Sergeant Major came, "Follow him," said Bluebell quietly. "Keep a watch on the boy and follow where he goes. Don't let anyone see you, especially him, and remember we know there are Greek Cypriots around. Just watch."

Half an hour later the Sergeant Major, happening to carry a pile of report books to the Officers' Mess tent, gave Bluebell a nod.

75

To Rifat's disappointment, Osman Ali—Rifat could not think of him yet as "Father"—could not eat. He drank greedily, thirstily and smoked a cigarette; when Rifat peeled the orange and offered it, Osman Ali sucked the juice but that was all he could do. "It's no good, son," he said. "I'm far gone." Then, "Could you take a message to Yalova?"

"Not a message," said Rifat, and he added, "There are Greeks all around. Yesterday our Captain turned off two patrols. It's not safe to stay here. The Greeks may find you. No, not a message," said Rifat. "Tonight, when it is dark, I'll take you home."

"How? I cannot walk."

"I have a donkey," said Rifat.

*　　　*

Luck favored Rifat's plan. It was Sergeant Major MacGregor's birthday. "Good old Pipes," said the men, and after supper they built a bonfire; sitting around it with their cans of beer, they had a "smoker" or singsong. Kip brought his guitar —Kip would strum it for two or three hours

76

together, his dreamy eyes more dreamy still—
and it was rumored that the Sergeant Major
was going to play the bagpipes. Bluebell, Lieutenant Thurston, and Second Lieutenant Moore
had come from the Mess tent to drink the
Sergeant Major's health; by "smoker" rules they
would each have to sing a song. Even the sentry
was leaning against the side of a truck, half
listening, and it was easy for Rifat to slip away
to Sippacik, undo her hobble cord, give her a
whack and a prick. Sippacik bounded in surprise

and set off at a trot. Rifat ran after her and called back to the sentry, "Donkey run away." The sentry let him go.

Away from the camp it was dark but there were stars and soon Rifat was able to pick out the track ahead and see the small dark shape of Sippacik. As he caught her he could hear the men singing to the thrum of the guitar.

"K-K-K-Katy, beautiful Katy,
  You're the only g-g-g-girl that I adore!
  When the m-moon shines, over the cowshed,
  I'll be waiting at the k-k-k-kitchen door. . . ."

and

"Kiss me good night, Sergeant Major,
  Sergeant Major, be a mother to me. . . ."

not at all the sort of English songs Hasan Dincer taught at school but they sounded cheerful and friendly and Rifat shivered as he looked across the silence of the dark *runda*—but he knew what he had to do.

Under his waistcoat he had four strips cut from his army blanket—with the first-aid kit scissors—he had not liked cutting the blanket but there was nothing else to do. Now he knelt and tied a piece over each of Sippacik's four hooves, muffling the plates so that they made no sound on the track; then, in this new quietness, he led her up to the cave.

He had to rouse Osman Ali, who seemed in a stupor, and then it was difficult to get him on to Sippacik's back. Rifat had not the strength to hoist him, but when Osman Ali had drunk a little water and Rifat had dashed the rest in his face, he managed, using his arms and hands for levering, to push himself up against the rock and so slide on to Sippacik's back. Putting his leg over her hurt him so much that a groan burst from him. "Try not to make a noise," Rifat whispered anxiously. "Be brave." It is usually a father who says that to his son but that night Rifat was in charge of his father.

Thin as he was, starved and losing blood, Osman Ali was a big and awkward weight on such a small donkey, especially as he could not balance himself and Sippacik's legs really did tremble but, as if she sensed the danger, she braced herself and did not resist when Rifat led her down from the cave across the valley toward the ridge of hills that separated the valley from Yalova. He did not use the track, but kept to little goat paths; they were steep and stony—but safer, thought Rifat. Osman Ali could hardly keep on; Rifat had knotted Sippacik's rope around her neck and Osman Ali held to that, his legs dangling, his head drooping so that Rifat thought he would fall forward. When the track went upward again, Sippacik kept having to stop, her flanks heaving, her breath puffing while Rifat's shoulder ached where he tried to keep it against his father's side, holding him up as best he could. The way seemed endless. Rifat thought hours of time must have gone as, a few steps at a time, a few yards, they went on under the stars, by those little devious goat paths that only Rifat knew.

Sometimes a stone rolled down, sometimes Sippacik blew, but otherwise there was silence until just as they came to the last ridge above the plain, Rifat heard voices. They were men's voices, subdued, but carried down on the wind. Rifat halted, tense. Yes. Men's voices. Tying Sippacik to a carob tree, he whispered to Osman Ali to put his arm round its stem and hold on, hidden by the branches, then he left them and crept forward to see.

A group of soldiers, five of them, Rifat counted, were sitting on the ground around a lantern that stood in a sheep pen made of cut furze and thorn. A sixth soldier was a sentry, his back turned as he kept a lookout over the track and the open land that lay between the ridge and Yalova. Rifat could see the village lights. Rifat, Sippacik, and Osman Ali would have to cross that open land, and in the bright starlight. By the dim glow of the lantern the five soldiers were playing cards—and they were talking—Greek.

Rifat wriggled back, a curious coldness on his neck where the sweat had broken out; the insides of his hands felt clammy; almost he had led his father right among Greek Cypriot soldiers, straight into an ambush.

Back at the tree he untied Sippacik—how glad he was that he had muffled her hooves—and led her and Osman Ali downwind, back down the ridge until he came to a small carob grove where one of the trees grew on a flat ledge, spreading its roots to hide a hollow below it; the tree itself cast a deep shadow. Rifat led Sippacik there, helped Osman Ali to slide down and crawl deep into the shadow, and whispered peremptorily to him to lie still. Rifat had made up his mind what must be done and, "I'll be back," he whispered. "Back soon." Osman Ali did not answer; his eyes were shut and a groan escaped him. Rifat led Sippacik apart, took her halter off, unwound the strips of blanket from her

81

hooves, and hobbled her tightly; if the Greeks found her in a halter and tied to a tree they would be suspicious, but hobbled, they would only think she was a donkey wandered from the village. "Don't go far, not far," Rifat whispered to her and he whispered an endearment, "*Sevimli, eşeğim.* Look after him." Rifat knew it was absurd to ask a donkey to look after his father but somehow it comforted him and Sippacik put back an ear, as if she heard and understood. He gave her a hug and a pat; then, as fast as his legs could carry him, he ran back to the camp.

*   *

"Sir! Sir! Captain Flower, sir."

The torch shone into Bluebell's face. He sat up on his camp bed, dazed.

"The Captain! Captain!" Rifat had shaken the sentry as he spoke. "Quick! Me, the Captain. Quick! Oh, quick!"

"He seemed so urgent, I thought I should wake you, sir," Gunner Smith said apologetically to Bluebell. "Can't make out what the trouble is but hope I did right." Before he could finish, Rifat was pouring out his story and soon Gunner

Smith was the one man in the camp—except
Sergeant Major MacGregor perhaps—who knew
for certain that Bluebell did speak Turkish.
Two or three times the Captain interrupted Rifat
with questions and the quick Turkish went back-
ward and forward in the small tent. Then,
"Light the lamp, Smith," said Bluebell, and
when it was lit, he sat perfectly still while the
flame wavered, and shadows moved over the
canvas.

Rifat moved too, from foot to foot, fidgeting
with impatience, wondering when the Captain
would speak. Do something, thought Rifat in

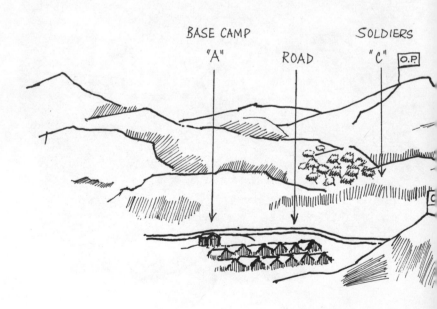

BASE CAMP   SOLDIERS

"A"   ROAD   "C"   O.P.

anguish. Once he said aloud, "Sir . . ." but Bluebell hushed him with a lift of his hand. Then,
"Pass me my map board over there on the
table," said Bluebell, "and the box of pencils."

As Rifat and Gunner Smith stood by, Bluebell
made marks on the map with his special indel-
ible pencil, shooting questions at Rifat, to ask
again where the ambush was, where the carob
grove, the tree with the roots on the ledge. "See,
here is Yalova," Bluebell told Rifat. "Here is
the camp." He marked it with his pencil. "Here
is where you left your father. . . ." Rifat's eyes
grew bigger as he looked at this wonder map. At

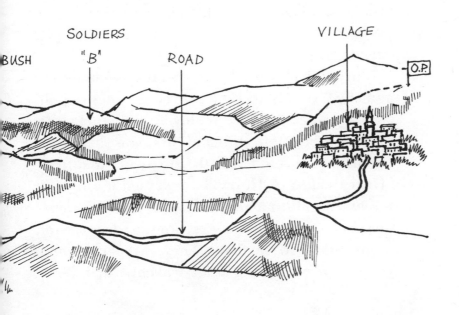

last Bluebell said to Gunner Smith, "Call Mr. Thurston and Mr. Moore; ask them to get dressed, and tell Sergeant Major MacGregor I want to see him—now. Then start waking the rest of the Battery; tell the Battery Quartermaster Sergeant I want tea for everyone in twenty minutes."

As Rifat heard the word "tea"—and he could not have been in a British soldiers' camp for a day without learning it—his worries broke. "Sir, not tea!" he begged. "Please, not wait for tea. Oh, hurry! Hurry! My father dying! They kill him if they catch him." Tears were running down his face, but Bluebell put a hand on Rifat's shoulder and said, "The best way to do things quickly is to do them properly. Now get outside while I dress."

Bluebell had been sleeping in his underclothes and shirt; it only took him three minutes to pull on his trousers, a thick pullover, and scarf—the night had begun to chill and Rifat was shivering, not only with cold but with impatience and fear. "Hurry! Hurry! Hurry!" he wanted to call and it seemed to him hours, though it was only minutes, before the other officers appeared, Sergeant Major MacGregor first. They were cold and grumpy from having been wakened and Bluebell poured them a whisky each; they drank it as they stood around his table where the map was now spread out. The camp was marked "A."

"This is a test exercise for the Battery," said Bluebell—he gave a quick look at the Sergeant Major—"to see how long it will take to get the men up and organized for a surprise night mission; then we'll carry out a simple approach march ending in an attack. You will need your maps. You, John," he said to Lieutenant Thurston, "will act as enemy and you will set off first. They are 'brewing up' now so tea should soon be ready. You can use transport, traveling with your lights on down the track, and set up a defensive position here." Bluebell marked the map "B" and Rifat could see it was high up on the ridge beyond the carob grove and his father's ledge and beyond the Greeks. "The rest of the Battery will be formed as two troops, one under you, Ted," said Bluebell to Second Lieutenant Moore, "will stay in camp. The other, under me, will march to this area, 'C.' " Again he marked the map: C was a position well to the right of the carob grove and below the Greeks. "We shall be seen in the starlight from B and will be fired on. I want to see how the N.C.O.s and men react. Sergeant Major, see that everyone has plenty of blank ammunition, Verey lights, and thunderflashes. We want a good show from both attack and defense, with a lot of sound and flashes."

"Very good, sir," said the Sergeant Major; it was possible that one of his eyelids moved in a vestige of a wink.

"It's now a quarter of an hour after midnight," said Bluebell. "In half an hour the defensive party should have left; it's only a couple of miles to B, so by one-thirty you should be preparing your position, John, and getting ready to defend it. By then, our troops should be on the move, so that by two o'clock we should be deployed over hill C and ready by two-thirty at the latest to get the attack under way. Our radio communications will be as follows . . ." but Rifat lost the rest of Bluebell's orders as, gazing at the map, he began to understand the plan.

When the officers had gone, Bluebell made it completely clear. The mock attack would impinge from both sides directly, though as if by mistake, on the Greek Cypriot ambush—"After all," said Bluebell, "they shouldn't be there"— the noise and lights would be all around them and would hold all their attention, "so that you and the donkey can slip out with your father; and if you go this way," said Bluebell, making circuitous dots on the map, "keeping to the low ground and well off any track, no one will see you. When you reach the open ground, go as fast as you can, but with the attack in full swing I guess the Greeks will be too busy to see you; with any luck they may have bugged out. Do you understand?"

Rifat had no need to answer. His face showed he did.

"Take this," said Bluebell, and handed Rifat some chocolate and the remains of a bottle of brandy. "Eat the chocolate and take a swig yourself; it will warm you and help you to run. The rest is for your father. Now get back to him as fast as you can and lie low until you hear us. Whatever you do," said Bluebell, "don't move until you hear the attack; a few shots won't do; wait for the full blast. Good luck," and with a squeeze on the shoulder and a push, he sent Rifat out of the tent.

＊　　　＊

No one saw Rifat run, a swift shadow, through the camp, and no one but the Sergeant Major knew there was a life and death reason behind the night exercise.

"Night exercise. Night exercise!" grumbled Garnett, "an' without a word of warning. What the heck's got into Bluebell now?"

"Should have written you a letter, shouldn't he, darlin'?" jeered Spud.

"Flipping silly nonsense," said Garnett, struggling with his puttees.

"Go and tell him so," said Spud.

"Here, have a cuppa,'" said kindhearted Kip, handing Garnett a cup of tea.

"Yes, darlin'," crooned Spud. "That'll make you feel better. I don't think!" said Spud and dodged as Garnett threw a mess tin at him.

*   *

Rifat found Sippacik easily; as if she had suddenly grown wise she had stayed in the carob grove. She gave a little whicker of welcome when she saw him and Rifat put a quick hand over her nose and dropped to the ground, holding his breath with fear; but no one in the ambush moved or spoke. Rifat put Sippacik's halter on, released the hobbling cord, blanketed her feet again, then led her to the hollow where Osman Ali lay.

At first Rifat thought his father was dead, he was so still and cold, but as Osman Ali felt Rifat's touch he put out his hand. "Son?" It was a thread of a whisper.

"Baba," whispered Rifat back. Baba is Turkish for father—it was the first time Rifat had used it. "Drink, Baba, drink," and he held Bluebell's brandy to Osman Ali's lips. Osman Ali swallowed a little, then Rifat lay down beside him, trying to warm him with his body while he held Sippacik with one hand, the halter rope lashed round her nose in case she whickered again.

Bluebell had said it would be two hours before the attack began but it seemed two years to Rifat. With the tiredness of his legs and the swig of brandy he had drunk, he would have fallen asleep but the jerk, jerk of Sippacik's rope kept him awake. The little donkey could have objected—after all, why should she not graze?—but again as if she sensed the danger, she stood above them, only moving her head; it was comforting to Rifat to see her furry, pointed ears against the stars. Then she was completely still, as if she had fallen into a doze and Rifat, with a little warmth creeping into him too as he warmed his father, dozed as well.

He was wakened by a spatter of shots. They were followed by more. At once he heard voices break out among the Greek Cypriots above him, a babble, though hushed, of annoyance and surprise; then it was lost as bedlam broke out on the hill. It was a bedlam of rifle fire, the "tacktack" of machine guns: of thunderflashes exploding and strange colored glares as the Verey lights went up, casting weird patches of light and shadow over the hills. Sippacik plunged and reared with terror so that Rifat could hardly hold her, but he quieted her and steadied her. Then he whispered to Osman Ali, "Now."

Osman Ali did not move, and Rifat shook him. "Baba! Father! Father, get up. It's time," but though Osman Ali woke with a start he could not get up. He tried to raise himself against the rock, Rifat holding him under the arms, but he was too weak. Once more he drank a gulp of brandy but still he could not get upright. Then how, how, thought Rifat, could his father get on Sippacik's back? Then, "Bring her," whispered the hoarse voice. "Bring her close. Make her kneel."

It is not easy to make a donkey kneel, especially when the donkey is frightened. Rifat led Sippacik close but she stiffened her legs as he tried to press her down. He pressed and pressed, and tried to break her stance by kicking her feet but Sippacik stayed planted firm. At last Osman Ali reached out and with a tremendous effort lifted her right fore foot; Sippacik wobbled, Rifat pressed, and Sippacik's legs collapsed. Hastily Rifat sat on her.

How lucky it was that he had often done this in the field or the shed. Now that she was down, Sippacik was placid and Osman Ali was able to drag himself close, and slide his leg over the small mound of her back while Rifat slid off. That was not difficult but they had to get her up again. "Up! Up!" coaxed Rifat's whisper through the noise of the attack. Sippacik tried; she heaved but Osman Ali was too heavy. "You must get up. You must," Rifat told her, through his teeth.

It was like a nightmare. All around them was the din of the attack, the soaring lights, and they who should be gone by now could not move. Suddenly a thunderflash went off even closer, deafening Rifat and giving Sippacik such a fright that she got up on her front feet. Quick as the flash itself, Rifat bent himself double and crawled under Sippacik, arching his back under her belly, adding his boy's strength to hers. Osman Ali, whose feet were still on the ground, pushed with them though sweat ran down his

face and a dark wetness gushed where his wound had opened again. There was a heave and a struggle and Sippacik was up on all fours, her legs tottering, her breath blowing through her nose, but up! Up, and Osman Ali was still on her back. Rifat wound the halter rope around her neck again, waiting for her to recover; they were ready to go down the hill, following Bluebell's dots, when Rifat stopped and froze to stillness.

Not fifty yards from him the Greek Cypriot soldiers were stealing down a defile, their lantern out. Rifat heard a man slide, a smothered curse, a few peremptory words—orders from the leader, thought Rifat. Rifat's hand tightened on Sippacik and he held his breath; it seemed impossible they should not see a donkey, a boy, and a man shadowed only by a carob tree, but Bluebell was right: the Greek soldiers had eyes and ears only for the attack and, "Aie! Did the British make a fine attack!" Rifat told the village boys afterward. He waited until all sight and sound of the men were gone, then he turned to look at his father. Osman Ali's hand was still on the rope; clenching his teeth, he nodded his head.

There was only half a mile to go, even by

Bluebell's circuitous route, but Rifat began to wonder if they could last that half mile. Osman Ali swayed dangerously on Sippacik's back; blood was seeping down from his wound; if he fell off now, Rifat could never get him up again. The Verey lights that rose and fell cast patches of dazzling brightness over the hills; when they burnt out, the darkness was blinding. Sippacik did not like it; she tried to stop; once or twice she stumbled and Rifat had to catch and steady them all. The noise of the attack reverberated in his ears, making a curious pounding, while his heart felt as if it would choke him. He had to trust to Sippacik to follow the goat path; he could no longer see it. "On! On!" he urged her. Sippacik gave a little spurt—and they came around a rock straight into a group of men.

"Greeks!" Rifat's heart gave a sickening lurch.

"For nothing! For nothing!" The cry went up in him though he made no sound. For nothing the escape with Osman Ali: the frantic run back to the camp: the daring of the sentry and then of the Captain: Bluebell's magnificent attack: the heaving up of Sippacik: the retreat of the ambush. He, he, Rifat, had led Osman Ali straight into another. They were caught. Then a voice called softly out of the darkness: "Kim O? Who is that?"

Turkish! And a voice Rifat knew well; Hasan Dincer's, the schoolmaster's.

Rifat had never thought he would be glad to see the schoolmaster but he gave a shout of joy. Next moment a hand was clapped over his mouth. "Sssh! Dunderhead! Do you want to bring them all down on us?"

"They're gone," and, the whispered words tumbling over one another, Rifat began to tell his tale but the schoolmaster cut him short.

"Tell us in the village." Already the whispered magic of the words "Osman Ali" had gone from mouth to mouth; two men supported the swaying man as, with the sound of the attack fading, Sippacik, almost trotting now as she smelled home, crossed the open space under the stars with her big burden, straight to Yalova and Arif Ali's house.

*   *

In the midst of the joy and excitement—Grandmother and Suzan weeping with gladness, getting hot water: sending a messenger off on a motor scooter for the doctor: making coffee for the men: Nazihar crying because she had been wakened to a turmoil of noise and excitement as Rifat told his tale—Sippacik staggered into her own little donkey shed where her legs collapsed under her and she lay down beside Siyergar. Presently Arif came out and gave her a long drink of water, an oke of barley all to herself, and a grateful pat. When she had eaten, Sippacik slept.

Nazihar came out too; she was sleepy but could find nowhere to sleep because the room was still full of excited men, all talking, making too much noise, and everyone was too busy to attend to her. When she saw Sippacik, Nazihar gave a cry of delight. She stroked Sippacik and patted her but Sippacik was asleep. Nazihar lay down on the straw, snuggled into Sippacik, yawned; in a minute she too was fast asleep.

*   *

Dawn was streaking the sky when Arif called Rifat into the courtyard. "The donkey is United Nations property," said Arif. "You must take her back."

"Back?"

"Yes. We must be honest. You should have asked if you could take her."

"How could I ask? There wasn't time."

"We must be honest. You must take her back."

Rifat had been feeling a hero but now he quailed. "There may be Greeks."

"If there are, they won't hurt you," said the schoolmaster, who had followed Rifat. "They won't hurt a donkey and a boy," but Hasan Dincer knew, as they all knew, this might not be true; boys had been shot on both sides and, "Aie! Aie!" said Rifat and shivered.

He need not have worried; there was the
sound of heavy wheels, a loud engine, and a
truck swept into the village. Driving the truck
was Bluebell; beside him was the Sergeant
Major.

"I think," said Bluebell to Hasan Dincer when he had jumped down, "I think it would be better if I took our donkey and the boy back in the truck."

"Much, much better," said the schoolmaster.

Nazihar was gently lifted aside and put to sleep in Grandmother's bed but Sippacik was roused and, in the half light, two ropes were put around her; there was a block and pulley in the back of the truck and she gave a startled bray as she found herself lifted into the air—but before she could writhe and kick, she was in the back of the truck, Rifat beside her.

Arif held out his hand to Bluebell. "We are

rejoicing," he said, with simple dignity. Bluebell was equally dignified. "Long may you rejoice," and Bluebell wrung the old man's hand.

*   *

It was at dawn too that the Battery got back to the camp. "What d'you suppose that was all about?" asked Spud as they made a second "brew up," each getting a mug of steaming-hot tea.

"Just one of Bluebell's little whims to make life pleasant," said Garnett.

It was Kip who found out that it was not a whim.

When the truck got in, Rifat was just awake enough to hobble Sippacik and turn her free; then he found his camp bed, rolled himself in what was left of his blanket, and in a second was asleep. Later that morning Kip came, leading Sippacik to the Sergeant Major's tent. "Look here, sir." The Sergeant Major looked and, at first, could not see anything remarkable.

"The boy's asleep, sir," said Kip, "in a dead sleep, so I went to see to the donkey. Found her like this, sir. Couldn't think what she'd got on her coat, it was that stiff and sticky. I tried to wash it off sir, an' look." Kip showed the Sergeant Major a wet rag stained with red. "Blood, sir," said Kip, his eyes round. "Sippacik, she's covered in blood."

*   *

The island was quiet. There had been three weeks of peace and 27th Battery was ordered to leave Yalova, to break camp, pack up and go. "But how are we going to part those two?" asked the Sergeant Major, looking to where Rifat was sitting on the ground, leaning against Sippacik's legs and eating an enormous slice of bread, butter, and cheese; every now and then Sippacik put her head around and Rifat gave her a bite. "How are we going to separate Rifat and Sippacik?"

"It'd be crool," said Kip.

"Send the boy home and take the donkey to Limassol and sell her at auction," said Garnett.

"You've got a soft heart, haven't you, darlin'?" said Spud.

"She'll sell better there—nobody knows her—and she isn't the boy's donkey, she's ours," argued Garnett.

"If she isn't the boy's she ought to be," said the Sergeant Major. That was the feeling of the whole camp. Though no one had mentioned Osman Ali, nor the reason for the night exercise, nor the blood that had stained Sippacik's coat, nor Rifat's long night walk, mysteriously all the men seemed to know of them. Sippacik was a small heroine, Rifat a hero and the Sergeant Major went to Bluebell. "The men feel, sir, that we ought somehow to keep these two together."

"How, Sergeant Major?"

Sergeant Major MacGregor coughed. "Well, sir, we thought we'd raise a fund. The men will dip into their own pockets."

"Which means I'll have to dip into mine," said Bluebell. "That's what you're trying to tell me, isn't it? Very well," said Bluebell. "Here's five pounds to start it off. . . ."

Lieutenant Thurston gave two pounds, Second Lieutenant Moore gave one. The Sergeant Major gave three—some of the N.C.O.s were better off than the officers—and the men passed the hat. Spud took the collection and when he came to Garnett he looked him in the eyes. "C'm on, darlin'," he said softly. All the men looked at Garnett until, very slowly, Garnett put his hand in his pocket. "Flipping backmail," he growled. All the same he gave ten shillings.

Rifat rode into the village, not only on Sippacik but on top of the pad, the wooden saddle, the panniers, which, with the halter and rope, even the stick, Bluebell had handed to him and which were all tied on Sippacik's back. Nothing could be seen of her but her head and tail and legs.

The village boys ran out to welcome them. "Rifat! You've come back!" They ran beside him in a throng and the men in the café put down their coffee cups to stare.

"Rifat! Rifat! Your father, Osman Ali, is back," they called.

"I know," called Rifat, trotting along.

"Rifat, the blue berets are gone."

"I know," said Rifat.

"Then why are you riding their donkey?"

"She isn't their donkey. She's mine."

When he reached home, he rode into the courtyard and Arif came out with Grandmother, Suzan, and Nazihar. Nazihar ran to hug Sippacik. Suzan wailed, "They have sent the donkey back." Grandmother shook her fist, but Arif said, "Seytan! You have taken their donkey again." Without answering, his face aglow, Rifat held out a paper.

Bluebell had given it to him. It was written in Turkish but Arif could not read it and Suzan called to Osman Ali who came painfully limping out. Osman Ali read, as Rifat sat upright on Sippacik, his face glowing with pride. "It is signed by the Captain," Osman Ali told the family. "The soldiers have given to Rifat the donkey they bought from us."

* *

Arif was taking his lemon crop to market. In good heart, he and Suzan and Rifat had picked it; soon Arif would be able to sit as long as he liked in the café—"Rest my old bones"—because Osman Ali would run the farm. His wound had healed and already he could limp about the courtyard on a stick, but he would still not be free to move about the island; United Nations advised he must stay in Yalova. Osman Ali was content. "I shall be a farmer, like Arif," he said.

"And so will I," said Rifat—"Then there will be no more school," he could have said.

Now, on this sun-filled morning Arif brought Siyergar and Sippacik into the courtyard. He put the saddle on Siyergar, a pad on Sippacik, then loaded both with panniers of fresh, good-smelling lemons. He was just leading the donkeys away when Rifat appeared in the doorway.

"Dede. Grandfather."

"Grandson?"

"Dede." There was a sternness in the way Rifat said it and Arif stopped.

"Did you want something?" he asked.

"Yes," said Rifat and stuck his thumbs into the armholes of his old waistcoat. "Dede, you should *ask* before you take *my* donkey."